Michel Streich

Grumpy
Little King

The little king was grumpy.

The little king was always grumpy.
Every day and all day long.

The little king's advisers were worried. 'Your Majesty,'
they asked, 'why are you grumpy all the time?'

The little king exploded. 'I am fed up with being the little king of a tiny nation! I want to be a big king, important, powerful and rich! I want to be famous and rule over an enormous country!'

The advisers thought for a moment. 'Your Majesty,' said one of them, 'the best way to make your kingdom larger is to fight a war.' The other adviser agreed. 'Fight a war, and you will become world-famous!'

So the little king decided to start a war right away.

He called for his general. The general loved war, and together they started planning.

First, they needed an enemy. They picked the lanky king – he was the little king's cousin and ruled over a country not far away.

They bought ships, planes and tanks, and lots of guns and explosives.

They gave uniforms and rifles to all the men in the kingdom. The men used to be bakers and teachers and farmers and builders. But everyone was a soldier now.

The general drilled the soldiers to obey orders. The little king spurred them on. 'If you fight bravely,' he told them, 'I will give you a medal!'

Parades were held. Everyone was so proud and excited.
The crowds cheered.

The little king gave speeches. He told his people,
'Our enemy the lanky king is a monster. We must
fight him and his soldiers to the bitter end!'

Finally, the little king returned to his palace. He was happy. Soon he would have his war and become a big king. He would be famous, powerful and rich.

He gave the order to attack.

The two armies faced each other on the battlefield.
'For our king! For our king!' the soldiers shouted.
'Let us follow our king into war!'

But then they noticed that the little king was nowhere
to be seen!

They searched everywhere, but they could not find the little king. His enemy the lanky king was not on the battlefield either, so the lanky king's soldiers joined in the search.

'Where is our little king?' the soldiers grumbled. 'He wants to be rich and famous, but we do his fighting!'

Finally, a soldier spied him. The little king was at home in his palace, sipping a cup of tea!

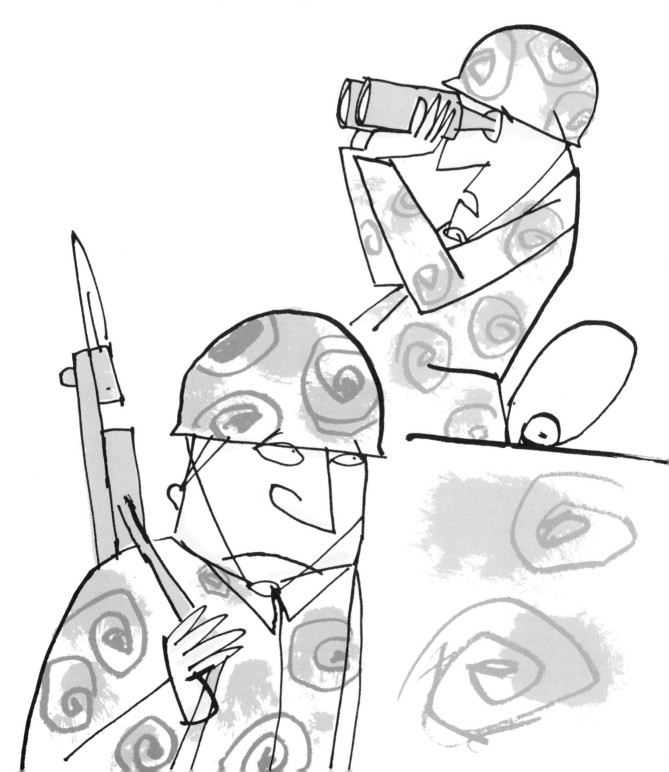

That was it! The soldiers were angry.
They dragged the little king to the battlefield.

And they fetched his enemy the lanky king as well.

They gave each king a rifle and told them both to fight,
just like everyone else.

But the kings were scared they would get hurt.
They were shaking with fear.

When the soldiers saw that the kings were cowards,
they packed up and went home. The war was over.

After all that, the little king was still little.
This made him very grumpy again.

But nobody cared.

Allen & Unwin
83 Alexander Street
Crows Nest NSW 2065
Australia
phone (61 2) 8425 0100
fax (61 2) 9906 2218
email info@allenandunwin.com
web www.allenandunwin.com

A Cataloguing-in-Publication entry is available from the National Library of Australia
www.trove.nla.gov.au

ISBN 978 1 74237 572 4

Designed and typeset by Michel Streich
Set in New Century Schoolbook 14.5/23 pt
This book was printed in July 2011 at Tien Wah Press (PTE) Limited,
4 Pandan Crescent, Singapore 128475

10 9 8 7 6 5 4 3 2 1